DARK NIGHT

by Dorothée de Monfreid

Random House  New York

Translation copyright © 2009 by Random House, Inc.
Translated by Whitney Stahlberg
Jacket art copyright © 2007 by Dorothée de Monfreid

Visit us on the Web! www.randomhouse.com/kids

Educators and librarians, for a variety of teaching tools, visit us at www.randomhouse.com/teachers

Library of Congress Cataloging-in-Publication Data
De Monfreid, Dorothée.
[Nuit noire]
Dark night / Dorothée de Monfreid. — 1st American ed.
p. cm.
Originally published: Nuit noire. Paris : l'école des loisirs, 2007.
Summary: When he wanders into the forest at night, Felix, terrified by the
ferocious animals he sees, finds refuge in an unusual underground house.
ISBN 978-0-375-85687-7 (trade) — ISBN 978-0-375-95687-4 (lib. bdg.)
[1. Fear—Fiction. 2. Night—Fiction. 3. Animals—Fiction.] I. Title.
PZ7.D3958Dar 2009
[E]—dc22
2008011257

MANUFACTURED IN CHINA
10 9 8 7 6 5 4 3 2 1
First American Edition

It was a dark night.

Felix was walking through the forest.
He was very little and very scared.

Suddenly . . .

AHOUOUHOU!

Felix stopped and stood very still.
"What was that?" he wondered.
Quickly, he found a hollow tree and tucked himself inside.

It was a wolf!
Felix trembled as he watched the wolf build
a great big fire and sit down in front of it.

"Stay still," Felix told himself.
And then, suddenly, he heard . . .

GRRRR!

The wolf jumped up.
Felix covered his eyes.

When he dared to peek, he saw that the wolf had left.

There sat a tiger on the stump.

Felix began to sweat.

"That tiger looks ferocious!" Felix thought.
But suddenly . . .

RRRAAAAAH!

The tiger ran away as
a third creature appeared.

A crocodile!

Felix's knees began to shake. He curled up more tightly in the hollow tree. And then he felt something against his back.

Very carefully, Felix reached behind him and felt
something hard and round. It was a doorknob.

Felix opened the door and discovered a stairway.
"Where am I?" he asked himself.

The stairway ended in a tiny kitchen. Felix saw hot
chocolate on the table. He helped himself. It was delicious!
Before he finished, though, a noise made Felix jump. Right
in front of him, a door began to open. . . .

"A rabbit!" cried Felix.

"A little boy!" cried the rabbit. "What are you doing in my house?"

"There were ferocious beasts in the forest," explained Felix. "While I was hiding in a hollow tree, I discovered your house."

"So now what are you going to do?" asked the rabbit.

"I want to go home, but I am afraid to go back outside," answered Felix.

"I will go with you," offered the rabbit. He put on a long black cape, grabbed a suitcase, and walked toward the stairs.

Felix followed, and when they reached the top of the stairs, the rabbit pulled a mask from the suitcase. He put it on his head and hopped onto Felix's shoulders.

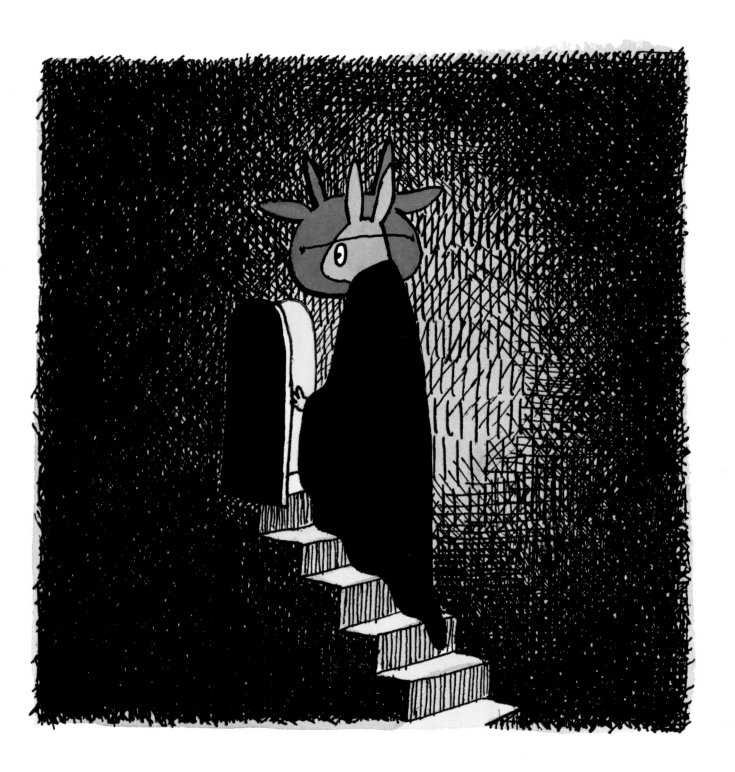

Underneath the cape, Felix trembled.

"Open the door, bend down, and head outside,"
instructed the rabbit.

Very slowly, Felix turned the doorknob.

"Walk straight ahead and growl like a lion,"
whispered the rabbit.

GRRROOOAHOU!

"Keep walking. And keep growling," said the rabbit.

GRRROOOAHOU!

At the edge of the forest, Felix called out, "There's my house!"
He began to run toward home.

He quickly opened the door and locked it behind them.

"Phew! That was close!" said Felix.
"We're safe," said the rabbit.
"I'm hungry," said Felix.
"Me too," said the rabbit.

Knock, knock, knock!

"Who's there?" asked Felix.

Voices from outside said, "Please open up!
There's a monster in the woods!"

"Just a minute!" called the rabbit.

"Hello," said Felix-the-monster as he opened the door.
"HELP!" screamed the wolf, the tiger, and the crocodile.

They ran away as fast as their feet could carry them . . .

. . . and disappeared into the forest.

"Now I'm *really* hungry," declared Felix.
"Me too," agreed the rabbit.

And Felix poured two steaming mugs of hot
chocolate, one for him and one for the rabbit.
"Cheers!"